RUSSIAN FOLK~TALES

RUSSIAN
FOLK ~ TALES

RETOLD BY JAMES RIORDAN

ILLUSTRATED BY ANDREW BREAKSPEARE

OXFORD

UNIVERSITY PRESS

OXFORD
UNIVERSITY PRESS

Great Clarendon Street, Oxford OX2 6DP

Oxford University Press is a department of the University of Oxford.
It furthers the University's objective of excellence in research, scholarship,
and education by publishing worldwide in

Oxford New York

Athens Auckland Bangkok Bogotá Buenos Aires Calcutta
Cape Town Chennai Dar es Salaam Delhi Florence Hong Kong Istanbul
Karachi Kuala Lumpur Madrid Melbourne Mexico City Mumbai
Nairobi Paris São Paulo Singapore Taipei Tokyo Toronto Warsaw
with associated companies in Berlin Ibadan

Oxford is a registered trade mark of Oxford University Press
in the UK and in certain other countries

British Library Cataloguing in Publication Data available

ISBN 0 19 274536 0

Typeset by Mike Brain Graphic Design Limited, Oxford

Printed in Italy by G. Canale & C. S.p.A. - Borgaro T.se - Turin

Contents

Vasilissa the Wise and Baba Yagá

There once lived an old man and woman with their daughter Vasilissa. One day, the woman called the girl to her bedside and told her this:

'Daughter, I am soon to die. Listen hard and heed my words.'

Thereupon, she took a little doll from under the covers and handed it to Vasilissa.

'Take good care of this doll and show her to no one. Whenever you need help, give the doll a bite to eat and ask her advice; she will tell you what to do.'

With that the mother kissed her daughter, closed her eyes, and breathed her last.

For a time the old man sorrowed and sighed, then sought another wife. The widow he married had two daughters of her own, two of the most spiteful, hard-to-please young madams that ever lived.

Because Vasilissa was so pretty, her stepsisters were extremely jealous; they and their mother were forever tormenting the little girl, making her work from dawn to dusk. How they wished her fair face to furrow in the wind, to roughen in the sun, to darken in the rain.

Yet Vasilissa bore all their taunts in silence and always had her chores finished on time. And while her stepsisters grew fat and ugly from being idle, she grew fairer still, not by the day but by the hour.

Of course, the little doll helped her all the while. Early each morning, Vasilissa would milk the cow and then, giving the doll some milk, she would say:

    'Little doll, little doll, listen, my dear,

      As I pour all my troubles into your ear.'

And late at night, when everyone was asleep, she would lock her door, rock the doll in her arms, and give her the scraps she had saved from supper. And she would say:

    'Little doll, little doll, listen, my dear,

      As I pour all my troubles into your ear.'

She would tell the doll how miserable she was, how her stepmother and sisters were always scolding her. The doll would first eat and drink, then comfort her with words of advice—and do all her chores. As Vasilissa sat in the shade, twining flowers for her hair, the vegetable beds were weeded, the fire was lit, the floors were swept, and the breakfast was cooked. All in the twinkling of an eye.

What is more, the doll also gave her herbs to protect her skin against the sun, wind, and rain, so that she became prettier than ever.

One day in autumn, the old man left for market and was not due back for several days. That night, when it grew dark, rain lashed the windows and winds howled beneath the eaves. To each of the three girls the stepmother set a task: the first she set to embroidery, the second to knitting socks, and Vasilissa to spinning yarn. Then, leaving a single birch splinter that flickered in the corner where the three girls sat, she went to bed.

For a time the splinter of wood spluttered and snapped, then suddenly went out.

'What are we to do?' cried the stepsisters. 'It is dark and we must finish our work; someone will have to fetch a light.'

Now, the wooden cottage stood on the edge of a dark wood in which lived a witch—Baba Yagá, cunning and sly, who gobbled folk up in the wink of an eye. Hers was the only house that would have a light.

'I'm not going to Baba Yagá,' said the first daughter. 'I'm doing embroidery and my needle is bright enough for *me* to see by.'

'I'm not going to Baba Yagá,' said the second daughter. 'I'm knitting socks and my two needles are bright enough for *me* to see by.'

'Then Vasilissa must go!' they yelled together.

So saying, they pushed their sister out of the house.

Poor Vasilissa went first to the barn, set some scraps before her doll, and said:

'Little doll, little doll, listen, my dear,
As I pour all my troubles into your ear.'

And she told the doll how her sisters were sending her to Baba Yagá's. The wicked witch would surely gobble her up. The little doll ate her food in silence, and her eyes began to glow like two bright candles.

'Never fear, Vasilissa,' it said. 'Keep me with you and Baba Yagá will do you no harm.'

So Vasilissa put the doll into her pocket and went off into the dark wood.

All about her trees rose up like towering giants. No moon, nor stars, shone in the sky above. All of a sudden, from out of nowhere, a horseman galloped past: his face was white, his cloak was white, his horse was white and its silver harness gleamed white in the forest gloom.

No sooner had he passed than the white light of dawn filtered through the trees. And Vasilissa walked on.

Presently, a second rider galloped past. His face was red, his cloak was red, his horse was red and its scarlet harness glowed bright in the gathering dawn. As he swept by, the red sun rose, kissing the girl with its warm rays and drying the dew in her hair.

She walked on through the forest all day without a rest, until towards evening she arrived at a small glade. And there in the middle stood a wooden hut on hen's feet surrounded by a fence of human bones crowned with skulls. The gateposts were dead men's legs, the bolts were dead men's arms and the lock was made of dead men's teeth.

Vasilissa stood still, rooted to the spot in fear. Just at that moment a third rider came galloping by. His face was black, his cloak was black, his horse was black and its harness loomed black in the gathering gloom. As he rode on, black night descended; and in the darkness the eyes of the skulls upon the fence began to glow like fire, lighting up the glade as bright as day.

Vasilissa shivered and shook, too scared to move. Yet worse was to come. Soon she felt the air tremble and the earth shake beneath her feet as out of the forest came Baba Yagá flying in a mortar, driving herself along with a pestle, and sweeping away her traces with a broom.

At the gate of the hut she paused and sniffed the air, her long hooked nose pointing towards the girl.

'Foo, Fee, Fo, Fum, I smell the blood of a Russian,' she cried. 'Who are you?'

'I am Vasilissa,' the girl replied. 'My sisters sent me for a light.'

'Ah, Vasilissa!' the witch shrieked. 'I know your stepmother right enough. So, you want a light, do you? Then stay and work for me, and we'll see what we shall see.'

Turning to her gate, she cried:

> 'Unlock yourselves, my bolts so strong!
>
> Open up, my gates so wide!'

As the gates swung open, she swept past in her mortar with Vasilissa close behind. And all was locked firmly as before.

Once inside the witch's garden, a birch tree went to poke out the young girl's eyes; but the witch cried out, 'Leave her be. It is I, Baba Yagá, who brings her here.'

At the door of the hut lay a fierce hound who went to bite the girl.

'Leave her be,' screamed the witch. 'It is I, Baba Yagá, who brings her here.'

Inside the door a big black cat went to scratch the girl.

'Leave her be,' yelled the witch. 'It is I, Baba Yagá, who brings her here. You see, Vasilissa,' she said, 'you cannot escape from me: my cat will scratch you, my dog will bite you, my birch will poke out your eyes, and my gate will bar your way.'

Baba Yagá then stretched herself upon the top of a stone stove, shouting loudly to the kitchen, 'Come, girl, bring me my supper.'

At that a black-eyed serving maid hurried in with food enough for ten grown men:

> A bucket of bortsch and half a cow,
> Ten jugs of milk and a roasted sow,
> Twenty chickens and forty geese,
> Two ox pies and cottage cheese,
> Cider and mead and home-brewed ale,
> Beer by the barrel and *kvass* by the pail.

Baba Yagá ate and drank greedily; and all that remained for Vasilissa were bones to pick and a crust to gnaw. As the witch got ready for bed, she said, 'Take this sack of grain and pick it through until not a husk remains; have it done by the time I wake up or I'll gobble you up!'

With that, she closed her eyes and began to snore and whistle, making the timbers shake.

Poor Vasilissa meanwhile took the crust of bread, put it before the little doll and asked her advice.

'Fear not,' said the doll. 'Say your prayers and go to bed; morning is wiser than evening.'

The moment the girl was asleep, the little doll called out in a clear voice:

'Pigeon, sparrow, chaffinch, kite,
There is work for you tonight.
On your help, my feathered friends,
Fair Vasilissa's life depends.'

The birds came flying in their flocks, more than the eye could see or the tongue could tell. They picked through the grain in no time at all: into the sack went the seed, into the bin went the chaff. And before the night was spent, the sack was full and the job was done.

Just as they were finishing, the white horseman galloped past: a new day dawned. When Baba Yagá awoke, she could not believe her eyes: all the work was done.

'I am going out,' she snapped. 'While I'm away, take that sack of black-eyed peas and poppy seeds, and sort it out. If it's not done by my return I'll roast you for supper!'

She opened the door, whistled shrilly and the pestle and mortar came sweeping up; in she stepped and was out of the yard in a trice, flying over the trees.

As she disappeared, the red rider galloped past and the red sun rose in the sky.

Vasilissa took a crust of bread to feed her doll and ask for help. And soon the doll's clear voice rang out:

'Come to me, you mice of house and field,
Sort through the seeds—or her fate is sealed.'

Mice came running in swarms, more than the eye could see or the tongue could tell. And before the day was out the job was done. Just as they were finishing, the black horseman rode past the hut and black night descended.

The eyes of the skulls began to glow like fire, the trees swished and the leaves quivered as Baba Yagá came sweeping in.

'Have you done all I said?' she cried.

'It's all done, Granny,' said the girl.

Baba Yagá was furious, but there was nothing to be done.

'Well then, go to bed, I'm going to eat my supper.'

While Vasilissa lay on rags behind the stove, she heard the witch talking to the black-eyed serving girl.

'Light the stove and make it hot; when I wake up I'll roast that girl in the oven.'

Whereupon, she stretched out on the stove, put her chin on a shelf, her nose on a bench, covered herself with her foot and began to snore so loudly that the whole forest shook.

Vasilissa began to weep and, taking the little doll from her pocket, put a crust of bread before her, saying:

> 'Little doll, little doll, listen, my dear,
>
> As I pour all my troubles into your ear.'

And the doll told her what to do.

Vasilissa went into the kitchen and curtsied low to the black-eyed maid.

'Please help me,' she said. 'When you light the stove, sprinkle water on the wood so that it doesn't burn well. Here, take my headscarf as reward.'

'Very well, Vasilissa,' replied the serving maid. 'I shall help you. No one has given me a present before. I'll tickle the witch's feet so that she sleeps more soundly, while you run away as fast as you can.'

'But won't the three horsemen catch me and bring me back?' she asked.

'Oh no,' said the maid. 'You see, the white horseman is the light of day; the red rider is the rising sun; the black rider is the dark night. They will not harm you.'

Reassured, Vasilissa went to run from the hut; but the big black cat flew at her and would have scratched her face had she not tossed it a pie.

As she ran down the steps, the dog darted out and would have bitten her had she not thrown it a bone.

When she dashed down the path, the birch tree tried to lash her face with its branches; but she tied them with a ribbon from her hair and the tree let her pass.

The gate would have swung shut had she not oiled its hinges with the morning dew.

Remembering the light for her sisters, she took a skull from the fence, stuck it on a stick and set off for home. The skull's eyes cast a piercing gleam before her, lighting up the way.

Meanwhile, when Baba Yagá awoke and saw the girl had gone, she screamed at her black-eyed maid, 'Why did you let her go?'

'Because she gave me her scarf,' the girl replied. 'I have served you all these years, and received only cuffs and curses in return.'

Turning to her big black cat, the witch screamed, 'Why did you let her go?'

'Because she gave me a pie,' the cat replied. 'I have served you all these years and never had as much as a crust from you.'

Into the yard rushed the witch in a fearful rage, shouting at her hound, 'Why did you let her go?'

'Because she gave me a bone,' the dog replied. 'I've served you all these years and never had even a scrap from you.'

'Birch tree, birch tree!' yelled the witch. 'Did you not lash her face?'

'No, I let her pass,' the birch tree said. 'For she bound my branches with a ribbon from her hair. I have been growing here these last ten years and you've never tied them even with a string.'

Baba Yagá hurried down the pathway to the gate.

'Gate, gate!' she screamed. 'Did you not bar her way?'

'No, I let her pass,' the gate replied. 'For she put dew upon my bolts. All these years I've served you, but you've never sprinkled even water on them.'

Baba Yagá flew into a fury. She beat the dog and the big black cat, she thrashed the black-eyed maid, chopped down the tree and gate.

She was so tired by then that she quite forgot about the girl.

In the meantime, Vasilissa ran home by the light of the skull; at dusk next day she finally reached the house, seeing that there was still no light within. Her stepmother and sisters met her at the door.

'What kept you so long, you good-for-nothing ragamuffin?' they all shouted at her.

And snatching the skull from her hands, they took it into the house. Yet then a strange thing happened.

The skull's glowing eyes fixed themselves upon the stepmother and her daughters and pierced them through and through. No matter where they tried to hide, the eyes followed them everywhere, burning, blazing, blackening, until they were reduced to cinders.

Only Vasilissa remained unharmed.

Next morning she took the skull and buried it deep beneath the garden; and in time a bush of dark red roses grew upon the spot.

That same day, Vasilissa's father returned from market and heard the story, from start to end. Truth to tell, he was glad to be rid of his evil wife and her two spoiled daughters.

And from that day on, he and Vasilissa lived in peace and comfort; and, of course, she kept the little doll safely in her pocket—just in case she might need her again some day.

Ivan the Fool and the Magic Pike

There once lived three brothers: two wise and one a fool. Ivan the Fool would sit upon the stove all day, sucking his thumb and dreaming dreams.

One wintry day, as the two elder brothers were getting ready for market, they told their brother to obey their wives while they were away.

'Do that and we'll bring you a pair of red boots,' they said.

The Fool grinned and lay back on the stove. As soon as his brothers had gone, the wives cried, 'Go and fetch water from the river.'

'Not I,' said he. 'It's too cold out.'

'If you don't go, we'll tell our husbands,' said they, 'and you won't have new boots.'

'Oh, all right then,' grumbled Ivan.

Down he climbed from the stove, pulled on his old coat and, taking two pails and an axe, went down to the frozen river. There he hacked a hole in the ice, scooped out two pailfuls of water and went to carry them home.

Yet when he glanced at the water, what a shock he got!

There was a big fish, a perky pike, swimming in one of his pails.

'What luck, I'll have fish soup for supper!' he exclaimed.

But he was startled to hear the fish cry out in a human voice, 'Let me go, let me go, and one day I'll repay you.'

Ivan the Fool only laughed.

'What good could you do me? Far better to take you home and eat you for supper.'

But the fish begged again, 'Let me go and I'll grant your every wish.'

'If I do let you go,' he said, scratching his head, 'you'll have to prove what you say. Make my pails walk home without spilling a drop of water.'

'Very well,' said the fish. 'You have only to say: "By will of the pike, do as I like!"'

Straightaway, Ivan the Fool said:

'By will of the pike, do as I like!

Off home you go, pails, all by yourselves!'

At once, the pails turned and trotted up the hill on little wooden legs.

Ivan slipped the fish back into the river and hurried after his pails. Meanwhile, the pails were marching down the village street, with people staring, open-mouthed, and Ivan following on behind, grinning all over his freckled face.

The pails went straight into the wooden hut and jumped up on a bench, while Ivan the Fool climbed back to the warm stove.

Presently, the wives cried, 'Go and chop some wood for the stove.' The Fool did not stir; he just muttered under his breath:

'By will of the pike, do as I like!
Axe, hop down from the shelf, chop wood
by yourself!'

No sooner had he uttered the words than the axe skipped down from the shelf, ran into the yard, and set to chopping wood. The logs filed into the hut one by one and leapt into the stove all by themselves.

By and by, the wives said, 'Go to the forest and fetch some wood.'

There was nothing for it but to climb down from the stove and pull on his boots. This time he took a length of rope and an axe, went into the yard and, climbing into the sledge, called out, 'Women, open up the gates!'

'What a ninny!' they cried. 'You haven't harnessed the horse to the sledge yet!'

'I can do without the horse,' he said with a grin.

So they opened the gates and Ivan shouted:

'By will of the pike, do as I like!
Sledge, race to the trees and do just as
I please!'

The sledge flew through the gates so fast, the two women tumbled over in the snow. It also knocked down many villagers on the way; they shouted angrily, 'Seize him! Catch him!' But the Fool paid no heed and only urged on the sledge even faster.

Only when he reached the forest did he halt the sledge and cry:

'By will of the pike, do as I like!
Show me more tricks and chop up some sticks!'

At once the axe began to chop wood, and the sticks dropped into the sledge one by one, binding themselves together in neat bundles. At last he climbed on top of his load and shouted:

'By will of the pike, do as I like!

Our work is done, off we go home!'

Once home, he settled back on the stove and went to sleep.

The days went by, whether fast or slow I do not know, but eventually the tsar came to hear of the Fool and sent a servant to bring him to the palace. When the royal lackey arrived at the village, he entered the brothers' hut and ordered the Fool to follow him to the palace.

But Ivan the Fool called down sleepily from the stove, 'Go away and let me sleep.'

At that the tsar's servant flew into a rage and struck him a blow upon the back. He was to regret it, for at once Ivan muttered:

'By will of the pike, do as I like!

Come, club, let the man know, what he's earned

for that blow!'

Up jumped a stout wooden club and beat the tsar's servant so hard it was all he could do to drag himself back to the palace.

The tsar was much surprised to hear what had happened; he now sent for his counsellor.

'Find the Fool and bring him here,' he ordered.

So the wise counsellor filled a basket with honey cakes, sunflower seeds, and bilberries and made his way to the village; he sought out the Fool's brothers and asked them what their brother liked best of all.

'He will do anything if you treat him kindly,' the brothers said, 'and promise him clothes of brightest red.'

The wise counsellor presented the Fool with the basket of food, saying, 'If you come with me to the palace, the tsar will dress you in bright red robes, a pair of red boots, and a red caftan.'

The Fool thought it over before replying, 'Very well, then, I shall come. But I shall make my own way when I'm good and ready.'

When the wise counsellor had gone, Ivan went back to sleep upon the stove; when he woke up, he raised himself on one arm and said:

'By will of the pike, do as I like!

Stove, full speed to the tsar, just as we are!'

No sooner were the words out of his mouth than the stove moved off by itself through the door, out into the yard and down the village street, heading for the palace—with Ivan the Fool sitting upon the stove.

As the stove was drawing near, the tsar looked out of the window and could hardly believe his eyes. He was at the palace gates as the Fool arrived.

'Look here, Fool,' said the tsar, 'I've had many complaints about you knocking down good citizens. I'm going to lock you up.'

Now, just at that moment, the tsar's lovely daughter, Princess Ludmilla, was standing at the palace window, watching the scene below. When the Fool set eyes on her, he fell in love at once; and he whispered under his breath:

'By will of the pike, do as I like!

May so lovely a jewel fall in love with the Fool!'

And he quickly added, 'Home, stove, as fast as you can.'

The stove turned and glided back over the snow towards his village; it entered the hut, stood in its old place, and the Fool went straight back to sleep.

Meanwhile, a great commotion had arisen in the palace. Princess Ludmilla had fallen sick, weeping and crying over her beloved. She begged her father to let her wed the Fool. The tsar was so furious that his daughter, the noble tsarevna, should wish to marry a foolish peasant that he told his counsellor to fetch the Fool forthwith.

Once again the wise man set off for the village with all sorts of cakes and sweet wines; once there he treated Ivan to the tempting food and drink. After the Fool had had his fill and fallen into a deep slumber, the counsellor put him into his carriage and took him back to the palace.

The angry tsar at once ordered a large barrel bound with iron hoops to be made. The two unfortunate lovers, Ivan the Fool and Princess Ludmilla, were put into this barrel and tossed into the sea.

When Ivan awoke, the princess told him tearfully of their fate. But Ivan was unafraid. He called out clearly:

'By will of the pike, do as I like!
Winds, blow the barrel to land, let it rest
on dry sand!'

A storm suddenly blew up, the waves raced over the sea and soon drove the barrel ashore. Yet even as they stepped from the barrel, the princess cried, 'But where will we live? We'll catch our death of cold upon the sand!'

To this Ivan replied:

'By will of the pike, do as I like!
Let a palace of gold, from the skies unfold!'

A gold-domed palace appeared from the sky and settled upon the sands, surrounded by leafy gardens with fragrant flowers and babbling birds.

The fair tsarevna and the Fool passed through the golden gates, wandered through marble halls and rested on satin couches. As she gazed fondly at her beloved, Princess Ludmilla sighed deeply.

'Oh, Ivan, if only you were not so plain, your nose was not so long, and your hair was not so red.'

It did not take Ivan the Fool long to decide.

'By will of the pike, do as I like!

A tall, fair, handsome man, no less, I'll be

to please my dear princess.'

And he became as handsome as the sky at dawn, the fairest man that ever was born.

Not long after, the tsar was out hunting when to his astonishment he saw a palace on the sands where none had been before.

'What scoundrel has dared to build a palace on my land?' he roared.

Ivan the Fool met him at the gates, led the tsar into the palace and seated him at a table groaning under a feast of food. The tsar dined and drank and marvelled.

'But what great tsar or duke are you?' he asked at last.

'Do you not recall the Fool who visited you on a stove?' Ivan asked. 'And do you not recall how you had him put in a barrel with your daughter, Princess Ludmilla, and tossed into the sea? Well, I am that same Ivan the Fool. If I choose, I can now send you and your entire tsardom to the bottom of the sea!'

The tsar raised his hands in horror and begged Ivan to forgive him.

'Take my daughter with my blessing, and half my tsardom too. Only spare my life, I beg of you,' he cried.

Ivan forgave the tsar and wed the fair princess. He then invited all the people to as grand a feast as Rus has ever seen. And when the old tsar died, Ivan the Wise became the best ruler Rus has ever known.

The Animals' Revenge

Catofay Ivanovich had been a fine mouser in his prime. But now that he was growing old, his master had no more use for him. So one day he took the cat deep into the forest and left him there.

Now, here's a fine to-do, thought the cat, his face as long as a fiddle. A lifetime of service and that's all the thanks I get: dumped in the forest, all alone!

Yet he was not alone. Two sharp eyes were watching him.

How can I profit from this? mused Lisa the fox. No forest creature has ever seen such a fierce-looking beast before.

'Hi there, cousin,' she called. 'You look as if you've fallen on hard times. If you like, you can move in with me; it's nothing fancy, mind, but it's dry and snug.'

'Thanks, I'm sure,' growled the cat, still out of sorts.

While the old tom-cat crawled into the fox's earth, Lisa dashed off to summon all the beasts of the neighbourhood.

'Bad news, friends,' she began. 'A new governor's arrived—a really frightful fellow: bristling whiskers, needle-sharp tongue, eyes that gleam in the dark, and claws like carving knifes. When he's asleep he snores like humans; when awake he just calls out "Mo-o-o-ore, mo-o-o-ore!" He's never satisfied.'

The beasts all oohed and aahed, squeaked and eeked.

'Mark this,' the fox continued. 'He's billeted on me, and he's already eaten me out of house and home. Now he wants you all to bring him food.'

Moans and groans echoed round the glade.

'Life's tough enough as it is, without a blooming governor,' complained Misha bear, scratching his stomach and shifting from foot to foot.

The animals went their separate ways, each with orders for the governor's table.

Next day they all assembled at the fox's home.

Levon wolf brought cheese and curds.

Misha bear brought home-brewed mead.

Baran ram had a basket of eggs.

Kuzma goat had a brace of pheasants, all plucked and cleaned.

Lisa poked her head out and held up a paw.

'Hush, friends, be patient, the governor's resting.'

'Hey, Lisa,' yelled Kuzma, 'go and wake him up. We haven't got all day!'

But she cut him short.

'Pardon me: be so kind as to address me as the governor's lady. Our new master has rewarded my loyal service by making me his lady wife.'

The animals glanced helplessly at one another, shrugged and fell silent.

Suddenly, Lady Lisa barked, 'Jump to it! The governor's coming. Quick, lay your gifts at my door.'

The beasts were too nervous to move. Each urged the other forward. Finally, it fell to shaggy old Kuzma goat who was so deaf he had missed most of the speech anyway. He shuffled forward, grunting, and hurriedly dropped his gift before the fox shooed him away.

Next came Misha bear. As he ambled forward and peered into the dark entrance, however, he caught a glimpse of a pair of fiery eyes lighting up a terrible whiskery face. On wobbly legs, he bowed repeatedly before making a hasty retreat.

'Make way, make way!' cried Lady Lisa. 'The governor is coming . . .'

That was more than they could bear; the animals all turned tail and fled into the trees and shrubs. Meanwhile, Catofay Ivanovich moved sedately into the clearing, his tail swishing fiercely; he stood before the feast laid out before him and set to gobbling greedily. Now and again, as was his wont, he gave a loud miaow:

'Mo-o-o-ore, mo-o-o-ore, mo-o-o-ore!'

As the cat was busy eating, Misha bear plucked up courage and poked his nose through the bushes to gain a better view. All at once, glancing sideways to the rustling leaves, the cat forgot himself . . . and pounced, thinking it was a mouse.

Poor old Misha nearly died of fright.

He took to his heels and shot through the trees like greased lightning, followed by all the others; they wanted to distance themselves as far as possible from the monster.

For a time the wily fox kept her mangy old lodger; but, having no further use for him, she finally sent him packing; and the cat wandered homeless through the forest until he stumbled upon a camp. It was the animals he had scared away.

'Brothers and sisters,' he cried, 'forgive me. I meant no harm. I'm no governor; I'm Catofay Ivanovich, an old tom-cat. It was Lisa who hatched the plan to be rid of you.'

One by one, the animals emerged from their hiding places to inspect the old cat; and when they saw he was harmless, they set to plotting revenge on the fox.

'I've an idea,' said Levon wolf at last.

When he had explained it to his companions, they all hurried down to the frozen river to fish. It being winter, they had to make a hole in the ice before dropping their lines into the water. Together, they managed to catch a sackful of fish—plump perch, catfish, and trout. These they took to a clearing close by the fox's house and they cooked them over a fire.

The smell of roasting fish soon reached Lisa's keen snout and she came to investigate.

'Well, hello there, friends,' she began. 'Spare a fish for your old friend.'

'Catch some yourself and dine to your heart's content,' said Levon wolf.

'If only I knew how,' replied the fox.

'Bless me,' sighed the wolf, 'there's nothing to it. Listen, sister, go to the river, drop your tail through the ice and shout: "Come to my call, fish big and small!" And the fish will come and hang on your bushy tail. But do be patient or you won't catch anything.'

So Lisa scuttered down to the frozen river, let her bushy tail through the ice and shouted: 'Come to my call, fish big and small!'

All night long she squatted there, and by morning her tail was frozen solid. When she tried to rise, she found she could not move.

'My, my, fancy that,' she chuckled. 'I've caught so many fish I can't pull them out.'

As she sat there stuck in the ice, wondering what to do, she suddenly spotted the animals coming with sticks, clubs, and clods of earth . . .

How they laid into the fox, and then tossed mud and rotten tomatoes at her!

Lisa squirmed and tugged with all her might; at long last, she tore herself free, battered and bruised, limping home across the snow.

That was how the animals gained revenge on the crafty fox.

Snowmaiden

It was midnight. The full moon cast a silver glow upon the wintry scene. Suddenly, the sky was full of birds returning from warmer lands and Spring in all her glory floated down to earth on the backs of swans and cranes.

'What a cold, uncheery welcome greets me here,' she said, landing in a fir-ringed glade. 'Winter has put the dancing brooks in chains, the meadows lie bare and barren, trees stand frozen in naked silence, amber resin hangs stiff on chilly trunks.'

She paused, glanced at the sky, and said, 'Above us in the clear night sky the moon and stars shine down in friendly greeting, while the sullen earth glints and gleams as hard and brilliant as a diamond necklace.'

As she was speaking, the birds around her shivered in the cold night air. Spring trembled too—from cold and shame.

'I am the cause of your suffering,' she said. 'Sixteen years ago I flirted with old red-nosed Frost. Since then he has held me in his power. I cannot go against him, for our daughter's sake. He keeps her deep in forest groves within his icy palace. It is because of her I fear to quarrel with old Frost. And so we suffer this long, cruel winter and late spring.'

Spring sighed, thinking of her daughter whom she loved dearly.

At that moment the giant figure of Old Frost strode out of the forest.

'Greetings, Fair Spring,' he boomed.

'And to you, Frost,' she replied. 'How is our daughter Snowmaiden?'

'She is well. I keep her with me in my ice palace; she is old enough now to need no nursemaids.'

'Old man, you know nothing of a maiden's heart,' Spring said crossly. 'She is sixteen; you should let her free to go wherever she chooses.'

'And what if the Sun should see her?' Frost asked. 'Should her heart be warmed by human love, she would melt away. Yarilo the Sun God would have her in his power.'

The parents went on debating their daughter's fate well into the night until, finally, a solution was agreed.

'A young girl does need proper care, I grant you,' said red-nosed Frost. 'But you, Fair Spring, have no time to guard her. We'll put her in the care of humble peasants who are old and childless. Snowmaiden will have so many chores there'll be no time for idle daydreams. Besides, no man will cast an eye on the daughter of poor peasants.'

Thus it was decided.

Next morning, two old peasants were out walking in the forest, gathering brushwood for their stove. It being the spring holiday, the old man was in good spirits, singing loudly and not altogether steady on his feet. His wife was not so happy: the sound of children's voices from the village pierced her heart, reminding her of their silent home.

'Cheer up, old girl,' said the old man with a laugh. 'I tell you what, let's make a daughter out of snow.'

The old woman grew angry at his foolishness.

'Have you no shame?' she shouted. 'What if folk see us playing such childish games?'

He ignored her grumbles and set to gathering piles of snow. First he rolled a snowball, then added arms and legs and, finally, placed a snow-head on snow-shoulders. He stuck on a nose and drew a mouth and eyes.

Then something happened that made the old pair gasp.

The snowmaiden's lips grew red, her eyes opened wide, she gazed fondly at the old pair and smiled a warm, grateful smile. Then, shaking off the snowflakes, she stepped out of the snow—a real, live girl!

The old man and woman stood back amazed. He fancied the drink was playing tricks with his eyes; yet his wife was staring too. At last, he found his tongue.

'What is your name, dear lady?'

'I am Snowmaiden,' she replied.

Without more ado, they led her to their cottage and, as they went, Snowmaiden turned to call, 'Farewell, father. Farewell, mother. Farewell, my forest home.'

Could it be the spring breeze rustling in the trees or did the old folk really hear voices from the forest calling, 'Farewell, Snowmaiden. Farewell, farewell, farewell . . .'

The trees seemed to bow to her as she passed and dense bushes parted to clear a way.

In the passing of time, Snowmaiden grew up not by the day but by the hour; and every day she grew more lovely than before. Her skin was whiter than the driven snow, her fair hair gleamed with a touch of ash or silver birch, her eyes were bluer than the frosty sapphire sky.

There was no end to the old pair's love of their daughter; they doted on her every minute of the day. And she grew up modest and kind. She did all the work about the home and, when she lifted up her voice to sing, the whole village stopped to listen.

Spring sunshine soon arrived to warm the land. Patches of green grass appeared amid the snowy wastes, and larks took up their woodland song.

Yet with the coming of the sun, Snowmaiden grew quite sad.

'What is it, daughter?' asked the old pair. 'Are you unwell?'

'All's well, mother. All's well, father,' she said in a whisper.

By and by, the first flowers bloomed, sprinkling the meadows with golds and pinks and blues. And all the birds of spring returned.

Snowmaiden grew quieter and sadder every day. She would hide from the sun, seek a chill shadow and stretch out her pale arms to the rain. Once a black storm-cloud burst, showering the village with hailstones as big as buttons. That cheered her up: she ran out to catch the hail as though it were precious gems. But, no sooner had the sun melted the hail than she burst into tears so bitter you'd think a sister was mourning her own dear brother.

One day, as summer was approaching, a group of village girls called on Snowmaiden to invite her out to play.

'Come with us,' they called. 'We are going to greet the summer.'

Snowmaiden shrank back into the shadows; but the old woman urged, 'Go on, daughter, go out and play with your friends. You should not stay at home with us old folk. Enjoy yourself in the sunshine.'

A village girl, Anna, took Snowmaiden by the hand, led her from the cottage out into the fields. Together they gathered flowers, plaited them into garlands for their hair, sang songs and skipped along the forest paths. The village was alive with merrymaking, and young men flirted with the happy band of girls.

Only Snowmaiden was sad. She walked alone, head drooping, no smile upon her frozen lips. But then, all of a sudden, she heard the lilting music of a flute; she glanced up and saw a humble shepherd boy standing before her, inviting her to join the dance. At first she refused, timidly hid behind the other girls, but the lad persisted.

'Dear Snowmaiden, come and join the dance. I'll play my flute for you alone; I'll put a happy smile upon your lips.'

Lel the shepherd was drawn to this lovely, timid maid and, now, gently took her by the hand. The other girls looked on in wonder as Snowmaiden whirled round and round with her merry partner. And slowly a pink flush of joy appeared upon her pallid cheeks.

From that day forth, Lel would often come to play his flute beneath her window, inviting her to walk with him through fields and meadows. Willingly the lovely, blue-eyed maiden ran out to greet her friend, went walking with him, made him chains of daisies and buttercups.

Though he grew to love her dearly, Lel felt no warmth within her heart; her friendship seemed as innocent as a child's.

One day, Lel was strolling alone down a woodland path when the beautiful, dark-eyed Anna came into view. Now, Anna had grown jealous of Lel's fondness for Snowmaiden and was ever seeking to turn his head her way. Finding him alone, she thought to try again.

'Oh, Lel,' sweetly she began, 'how glad I am to find you alone. My heart is overflowing with love: let me kiss your eyes and cheeks; let me warm you with my love.'

The young shepherd was soon overcome; the love that filled his own heart now poured forth. Just at that moment, Snowmaiden emerged from the trees and chanced upon the embracing pair.

She stopped, uncomprehending.

At once Lel broke away from Anna and ran to explain.

'You see, dear Snowmaiden,' he gently said, 'Anna's heart is warm and full, like mine. But yours is cold and empty. Why can't you love like her?'

With tears glistening on her pale cheeks, Snowmaiden turned and fled into the forest depths. She did not stop until she came to a deep lake mantled by pink-white lilies. The lake was encircled by blossoming shrubs and trees whose boughs overhung the shimmering water. Standing on the bank, she called out in a sobbing voice, 'Mother mine, in tears of grief and anguish your daughter speaks to you. I want to learn to love. Give me a human heart, I beg of you.'

Out of the lake slowly rose Fair Spring and gazed fondly on her sobbing child.

'I can spare you just one hour,' she said. 'For at daybreak Yarilo the Sun God begins his summer reign and I must depart for another year. What is it you wish, my child?'

Snowmaiden spoke one word.

'Love.'

Then, with a trembling sigh, she said, 'All about me everybody loves, all are happy and content. I alone am loveless: neither loving, nor able to love. Mother, I want to love, yet I do not know how.'

'Daughter,' her mother solemnly began, 'have you forgotten your father's warning? You well know that love could mean your death.'

'If that is so I'd sooner die,' said Snowmaiden. 'To love for a moment, however brief, is dearer to me than a loveless life.'

'So be it, my child,' Fair Spring sighed, unable to refuse. 'I shall share my love with you. The source of love lies in the crown of lilies on my head. Take it and put it on yourself.'

Joyfully, Snowmaiden took the crown of lilies and placed it on her own fair head. At once, she shouted out, 'What strange feeling beats within my breast? My eyes are opening to the beauty of the world; my ears can hear the joyous birdsong; my heart is full of the joys of spring.'

'My beloved child,' her mother said, 'the fragrance of spring has filled your soul. You will soon know the full power of love within your heart. But heed my words: guard your love from Yarilo's fiery gaze. Do not stay to admire the crimson rays of dawn; run quickly to seek the leafy shade and coolness of the wood. Farewell, my child.'

With those last words, Spring sank below the glistening waters of the lake.

Snowmaiden skipped along the woodland paths. Her love-filled heart beat faster as she caught the clear notes of a flute. Rushing towards the sound, she soon came to a sunny woodland glade. And there, upon a fallen log beside a tall fir tree, Lel the shepherd sat, playing his flute and looking very sad.

On seeing the girl he loved, Lel jumped up and cried out with joy, 'Snowmaiden, I have been searching for you all day. Please forgive me for those hasty words. You must be angry.'

'Oh no, Lel,' softly she replied. 'It is not anger that fills my breast. It is love. Now I know there is no more tender feeling in the world.'

'So you do have a heart, dear Snowmaiden,' said Lel. 'You do love me, after all.'

'I never shall stop loving you,' she replied.

At that moment she glanced up at the sky.

'We must hurry,' she said. 'Yarilo's rays already frighten me. Save me from them, Lel, for they cause me such pain.'

Lel frowned; he did not understand.

'Dear Snowmaiden, we cannot hide our love forever from the light of day,' he said.

As he was speaking, the radiant sun rose higher in the cloudless sky, dispersing the mists of dawn and melting the last trace of snow.

A ray of sunshine fell on Snowmaiden.

With a cry of pain, she tore herself from Lel and, in a hoarse whisper, begged him to play one last time for her.

Putting the flute to his trembling lips, he began to play a wistful tune. As she listened, tears rolled down her cheeks, colour drained from her lovely face, and her feet melted away beneath her.

Slowly her body sank into the damp grey earth, until all that remained was her crown of water lilies. A wisp of white mist rose up and up and vanished into the cloudless sky.

'Snowmaiden, dearest Snowmaiden,' cried Lel in despair. 'You begged me to protect you from the sun, but I would not listen. And now, before my eyes, you have melted like the last spring snow. Please forgive me.'

But no one heard his cry.

No one, that is, except a grieving mother in a lily-mantled lake, and old red-nosed Frost far away in the northern snows.

Fenist the Falcon

Long, long ago, there lived a wealthy farmer with three daughters. After his wife died, the youngest daughter, Marushka, said to him, 'Don't worry, father. I'll look after the family.'

And a fine mistress she made. But her two sisters were vain and lazy; nothing pleased them for long: not frocks or smocks, caftans or sarafans.

One day the farmer made ready for market and asked his daughters what gifts he should bring.

'Bring us each a rich silk shawl,' the elder girls exclaimed, 'with flowers in red and gold.'

Marushka was silent.

43

'And you, my child?' her father asked.

'Bring me a feather from Fenist the Falcon,' she said at last.

The farmer set off and later returned with the two shawls, but no falcon's feather— despite searching high and low.

Some months later he again made ready for market, asking his daughters what their wishes were.

'Bring us each a pair of silver shoes,' the elder girls cried.

But Marushka softly said, 'Bring me a feather from Fenist the Falcon, father.'

All that day the farmer searched high and low; he bought the shoes readily enough, but nowhere could he find the falcon's feather. So he returned without it. Once more his daughter comforted him.

'No matter, you will find it another day.'

A few months passed and, as he set out for market a third time, his two elder daughters said, 'Bring us each a saffron gown.'

But Marushka said softly as before, 'Bring me a feather from Fenist the Falcon, father.'

Though he asked at every booth and stall, the man could find no news of such a feather. On his way home, however, he chanced to meet an old, old man.

'Good morrow to you, brother,' called the old man. 'Whither are you bound?'

'Good day to you,' the farmer replied. 'I am returning home with heavy heart. My youngest daughter wants a feather from Fenist the Falcon, and I can find it nowhere.'

The old man smiled, taking a birch-bark box out of his pocket.

'I have the very feather you seek,' he said. 'It is a magic feather; but I know your daughter is deserving, and she shall have it.'

44

So saying, the old man gave the feather and its box to the delighted farmer. It looked to him exactly like any other feather, but he took it thankfully and went on.

On reaching home, he gave out his presents to the daughters. The two elder girls tried on their new gowns and mocked their foolish sister, 'Stick the feather in your hair and see how grand you'll look.'

Marushka just smiled and made no reply.

Late that night, when the household was asleep, she took the feather from its box, flung it to the floor and murmured low, 'Come to me, Fenist, my bright-eyed Falcon.'

And the feather turned into a bright-eyed young man, as handsome as the sky at dawn. The two talked together until first light; but then he struck the floor and took his falcon shape once more. As Marushka opened the window, he soared up into the sun-streaked sky.

For three nights she made him welcome. On the fourth night, however, her sisters overheard them talking in her room and, come the dawn, they watched the Falcon fly from the window.

That day, the two spiteful sisters stuck sharp knives along the window ledge in their sister's room. Marushka did not notice them as she went to bed that night.

As soon as dusk descended, the Falcon came and beat against the ledge until both his wings were cut by the sharp knives.

Marushka slept on, hearing nothing.

'Farewell, my fond love,' he sighed at last. 'If you love me truly you will find me, but it will not be easy. You must go to the ends of the earth; wear out three pairs of iron shoes and three iron staffs, and eat through three stone loaves.'

Through the mist of her slumbers, Marushka caught his words, sprang quickly out of bed and ran to the window. But it was too late: the Falcon was gone. All that remained were red drops of blood upon the window ledge.

Marushka wept long and bitterly, as if her heart would break; and her tears washed away the drops of blood.

Next morning, she went to her father, saying, 'Give me your blessing, father. I am going to seek my own true love.'

The man was heartbroken to lose his beloved daughter, yet he knew he must let her go. So, with his blessing, she ordered three pairs of iron shoes, three iron staffs, and three stone loaves. Then off she went on her long journey to the ends of the earth.

Over the open plain she walked, through dark forests and across tall hills. The birds cheered her with their song, the brooks washed her dusty feet, and the dark forests bade her welcome. No beast would harm her, for they knew she was an honest maid.

On and on she went until at last one pair of iron shoes wore out, one iron staff broke in two, and one stone loaf was eaten through.

Just then she emerged into a clearing in the trees: and there before her stood a little hut on hen's feet, spinning round, with no windows.

'Little hut, little hut,' called the girl, 'turn your back to the trees and your face to me, please.'

The little hut on hen's feet stopped spinning and in went Marushka boldly through the open door. Inside, on the great stone stove lay Baba Yagá, a bony hag with a long hooked nose and a single tooth that hung below her chin.

Marushka was not afraid. She told the witch about her quest, and begged her help.

'You have far to go, my pretty one,' said Baba Yagá. 'Fenist lives in a land far, far away. The queen of that land is a wicked sorceress who gave your Fenist a magic potion and, while the spell was on him, made him marry her.

'But I shall help you. Take this silver saucer and golden egg, and carry it with you to the palace; should the queen wish to buy it, do not sell until she lets you see Fenist the Falcon.'

Then Baba Yagá took a ball of golden thread, rolled it along the forest path and said, 'Follow the golden thread into the forest; it will lead you to my second sister, and she will help you further.'

Thanking Baba Yagá, Marushka continued on her way. The trees closed about her, the forest grew dark and owls hooted through the gloom. On and on she went until the second pair of shoes wore out, the second staff broke in two and the second loaf was gone. Just then she emerged into a clearing where a hut on hen's legs was spinning round and round.

'Little hut, little hut,' cried the girl, 'turn your back to the trees and your face to me, please.'

The hut came to a stop, windows and a door appeared, and in went Marushka through the open door. There on the great stone stove lay a second Baba Yagá, even more ugly and skinny than her sister.

Marushka told her story and showed the egg and saucer from the first witch.

'Very well, my pretty one, I shall help you,' said the hag. 'Take this golden needle and silver frame; should the queen wish to buy it, do not sell until she lets you see your Fenist. But first you must go to my older sister; she will help you further.'

Thanking the second Baba Yagá, Marushka cast the ball of golden thread upon the ground and followed it through the trees.

Now the branches and brambles caught at her sleeves and scratched her face, no birds sang and wild eyes watched her on her way. But she pushed on without a backward glance.

By and by the third pair of shoes wore out, the third staff broke, and the third stone loaf was eaten through. Just then Marushka emerged into another clearing; and again she spied a little hut on hen's feet turning round and round.

'Little hut, little hut,' she called, 'turn your back to the trees, and your face to me, please.'

The hut came to a halt and in she went through the open door. There upon the great stone stove lay the third Baba Yagá, the boniest and ugliest of them all.

Marushka told her story.

'Fenist the Falcon is not easy to find, my dear,' the old hag said. 'You have still to travel to the ends of the earth. But I shall help you. Take this silver distaff and golden spindle to the palace; should the queen wish to buy it, do not sell until she lets you see Fenist the Falcon.'

Thanking her, Marushka dropped the ball of golden thread upon the ground and followed it into the eerie forest. She had not gone far when she heard a roaring and a rumbling: owls fluttered and wheeled about, mice scampered beneath her feet, and hares hopped across her path. As she stopped in alarm, a big grey wolf appeared.

'Have no fear, Marushka,' the grey wolf said. 'Come, climb upon my back and I shall take you to the palace.'

She sat astride the wolf's broad back and off they sped like the wind after the ball of thread.

Green fields swept by in the wink of an eye, mountains so high they reached to the sky until, at last, they reached a crystal palace, its golden domes glittering in the sun. And there was the queen herself, staring down from her white tower.

Thanking the wolf, Marushka took her bundle and walked to the foot of the tower. She curtsied low and politely said, 'Pardon me, Your Majesty, do you need a maid to spin, weave, and embroider?'

'If you can do all three well, girl, then enter and set to work,' replied the queen.

So Marushka became a servant at the palace. She toiled without rest all through one day and, when evening came, she took her golden egg and silver saucer and showed them to the queen. At once the egg began to roll around the saucer and there came a ringing of bells; then, one after the other, all the great cities of Rus appeared in the saucer.

The queen was amazed.

'Sell me your silver saucer and golden egg,' she said.

'They are not for sale, Your Majesty,' Marushka replied. 'But you may have them for nothing if you let me see Fenist the bright-eyed Falcon.'

The queen agreed.

'Very well. Tonight, when he is asleep, you may enter his chamber.'

Night came and Marushka hurried to Fenist's bedchamber, finding him fast asleep. He could not be wakened, for the cunning queen had stuck a magic sleeping pin into his shirt. No matter how hard Marushka called him, kissed his dark brow, and caressed his pale hands, he slept on without waking. As the rays of morning light shone through the window, she still had not roused her beloved and she had to leave.

All that day she toiled without cease and in the evening took out her silver frame and golden needle; as the needle worked away she murmured to herself, 'Embroider a cloth for Fenist to wipe his brow on each morning.'

Once again the queen was shown the frame and needle, and wished to purchase them at once.

'I will not sell,' Marushka said, 'but you may have them for nothing if you let me see Fenist again.'

The queen agreed.

'Very well, you may see him tonight.'

As night fell, Marushka entered the bedchamber and found him deep in slumber.

'Oh, my Fenist, my bold, bright-eyed Falcon,' she cried. 'Wake up and speak to me.'

But he slept on soundly, for the cunning queen had left a magic pin in his thick hair as she had combed it; and Marushka could not rouse him, however much she tried.

At daybreak, she had to give up in despair and depart. That day she laboured without pause and, when evening came, she took out her silver distaff and golden spindle. The queen once more asked to buy them, but Marushka repeated, 'They are not for sale. But you may take them if you let me see Fenist the Falcon one last time.'

'Very well,' agreed the queen, knowing that Marushka would not be able to rouse him—for she had drugged him with a sleeping potion.

Night drew on and Marushka went to the chamber for the final time. But Fenist was deep in slumber as before.

'Oh, Fenist, my bold and bright-eyed Falcon, wake up, wake up,' she cried out in despair.

Fenist slept on through the night. And though she tried again and again to rouse him, it was to no avail. When it was almost dawn she stroked his dark hair as she said her last farewell.

A hot tear rolled down her cheek and fell upon his shoulder, burning the tender skin.

Slowly he stirred and opened his eyes. Seeing Marushka, he at once sat up.

'Can it be you, my long-lost love?' he cried, tears of joy coming to his eyes. 'So you have worn out three pairs of iron shoes and three iron staffs; you have eaten through three stone loaves. To the ends of the earth you have journeyed. Nothing can part us now.'

With the spell upon him broken, Fenist brought Marushka before the royal court. The boyars consulted and gave their verdict: the old queen was to be banished from the land; Marushka would take her place.

For she was bold and wise and strong.

The Flying Ship

There once lived an old peasant and his wife with their three sons. The two eldest were clever and hard-working, clean and tidy; but the youngest was a fool, a grubby, idle scallywag who was forever lounging about in the hay.

One day, news came to the village that the tsar had issued a grand proclamation:

> BY ROYAL COMMAND
> A FLYING SHIP IS
> TO BE BUILT

Whoever succeeded in doing so would be rewarded with half the realm—and the royal princess into the bargain.

The two eldest brothers made up their minds to try their luck. With their father's blessing and a knapsack of white bread, cheese, and wine, they set off to build a flying ship.

Soon after, the Fool thought to try his luck too.

'Don't be daft,' said his mother. 'If you wander off the wolves will eat you or you'll fall into a ditch. Just you stay at home.'

But there is no reasoning with a fool. Once he had got it into his head that he would build a flying ship, he would not budge. He so pestered the old folk that in the end they were glad to see the back of him. Taking a bag of burnt rusks and a flask of plain water, he went merrily on his way.

He had not gone far when he came upon an old beggar by the wayside.

'Where are you heading, young sir?' asked the beggar.

The Fool told the story of the tsar's command and the big reward.

'But can you really build such a ship?' asked the beggar.

'No, I cannot,' replied the Fool.

'Then why are you going?' asked the man.

'Goodness knows,' said the Fool with a toothy grin.

'Well, if that's the case, you're in no hurry. Come, let's take a rest and have a bite to eat. What's that in your bag?'

The Fool was a mite ashamed to share his poor fare; but the beggar was not choosy.

'Never mind how poor it is; what God gives we must be thankful for.'

So the Fool untied his bundle . . . What was this? Instead of black rusks, he found crisp white rolls and all manner of tasty sweetmeats.

'You see how the good Lord takes pity on a Fool,' said the beggar. 'Come now, let's have a drink.'

The Fool was even more surprised to find that the water in his flask had turned to wine. He willingly shared that too. After the meal, the beggar told how he had also met his brothers; but they had refused to share even a crust with him.

'For your kind heart you shall be rewarded,' he said. 'Heed my words well: go into the forest and stop at the first tree, cross yourself three times and strike the tree once with your axe. That done, quickly throw yourself to the ground, cover your face and sleep till dawn. At first light you will see before you a splendid ship; climb into it and fly off wherever takes your fancy. However, mark my words: you must take on board every wayfarer you pass.'

Thanking the beggar, the Fool continued on his way. When he came to the forest, he went up to the first tree and carried out the old fellow's instructions to the letter: crossed himself three times, struck the tree with his axe, fell to the ground, covered his eyes and

went to sleep. He was woken by the first rays of dawn. And there before him stood a magnificent ship! No sooner had he climbed on board than it rose up into the air, soaring high above the treetops. He flew over meadows and seas, forests and leas, and mountains so high they reached to the sky.

All of a sudden, however, he spied a man far below kneeling on the ground, his ear pressed to the earth.

'Ahoy there, matey,' shouted the Fool. 'What are you doing with your ear pressed to the ground?'

'I'm listening to news from far and near,' hollered back the man. 'My hearing is so keen I can hear all that is happening in the world.'

'Why don't you join me in my flying ship?' cried the Fool, bringing the vessel down alongside the kneeling man.

The fellow readily agreed, climbed on board and off they flew into the clear blue sky. They had not flown far when they saw a man hopping on one leg with the other tied to his ear.

'Ahoy there, matey,' shouted the Fool. 'Why are you hopping on one leg with the other tied to your ear?'

'Because if I didn't,' replied the man, 'I would step halfway across the world in no time at all.'

'Why don't you join us in our flying ship?' suggested the Fool, bringing it down to land.

The fellow on one foot hopped into the ship and off they flew again over forest and plain until they spied a man shooting his gun at nothing at all; there was no bird nor beast in sight. The Fool steered his ship down and asked the man why he was aiming his gun at the sky where there was no bird in sight.

'I am so long-sighted,' sighed the man, 'I can see only birds and beasts a thousand miles away.'

'Then come and join our crew,' said the Fool.

When he was safely on board the flying ship, the Fool cast off and

the four were soon soaring through the clear blue sky. On and on they sailed until they saw a man below carrying a huge sackful of loaves on his back. The Fool steered the ship until it was level with the man.

'Ahoy there, matey,' he called. 'Where are you going with such a load?'

'I'm on my way to town to buy bread for dinner,' replied the man.

The Fool was puzzled: 'But you have a whole sackful of loaves on your back!'

'That's nothing,' was the reply. 'I could swallow that in one go and still be hungry.'

'Come and join our crew,' called the Fool, landing his ship beside the hungry man, who eagerly accepted the offer and climbed aboard. And on they went. They had not gone far when they spied a man walking round and round a lake. When the Fool enquired what he was doing, the man called back, 'I'm thirsty, but I can find no water.'

'But there's a whole lake right in front of you,' said the Fool in amazement. 'Why don't you drink from that?'

'Alas, I'd swallow this lake in one gulp and still go thirsty,' said the man.

When the Fool invited the thirsty man to join his crew, he readily agreed. On they flew until they saw a man walking into the forest with a bundle of brushwood on his back.

'Hey there, matey,' cried the Fool. 'Why are you taking brushwood into the forest?'

'This is no ordinary brushwood,' called the man. 'I only have to scatter it over the plain and an entire army will spring up.'

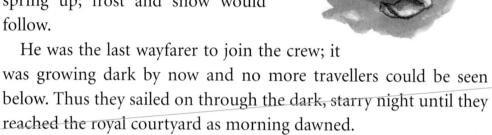

He, too, joined the crew, and next they came upon a man carrying a bale of hay— but no ordinary hay. No matter how hot the sun, he had only to spread the hay upon the ground and a cool breeze would spring up; frost and snow would follow.

He was the last wayfarer to join the crew; it was growing dark by now and no more travellers could be seen below. Thus they sailed on through the dark, starry night until they reached the royal courtyard as morning dawned.

They arrived just as the tsar was having breakfast. Seeing the flying ship landing on his lawn, he immediately sent a footman to enquire who the visitors were. On learning that not a single one was of noble blood—they were common peasants to a man—the tsar was most annoyed. How could he marry his daughter to a simpleton?

He scratched his head.

'What if I set some impossible tasks?' he mused. 'That will rid me of these knaves without going back on my word.'

So he sent an order to the Fool to bring him the Water of Life— before breakfast was done!

Now, while the tsar was informing his flunkey of this command, the first wayfarer (the one who could hear news on the other side of the world) caught the royal words and told the Fool.

'What am I to do?' wondered the Fool. 'I would not find such Water in a month of Sundays, let alone before breakfast is over!'

'Never fear,' said Giantsteps. 'I'll fetch it in a trice.'

And as the flunkey brought the royal command, Giantsteps was already unhitching one leg from his ear and speeding off to collect the Water of Life. He had a full flask before you could say Ivan Ivanovich.

There's no rush, Giantsteps thought to himself. I'll just take forty winks beneath this windmill before I return.

And off he dozed.

Back at the palace, the tsar was just finishing his pancakes and caviare; and the shipmates were becoming uneasy. The first wayfarer, Big Ears, put his ear to the ground and heard the snores beneath the windmill; Crackshot took his gun, fired at the windmill and woke up Giantsteps, who brought the Water back in the nick of time—just as the tsar was rising from the table.

Foiled on the first task, the tsar now set a second: to eat a dozen roast oxen and a dozen freshly-baked loaves at a single sitting. This was more impossible than the first, he thought.

'I could not eat a single ox in one meal,' groaned the Fool.

'Don't worry,' said the Hungry Man. 'That's not enough even to whet my appetite!'

And he devoured the twelve roast oxen and twelve freshly-baked loaves in one gulp—and then called for more. The tsar was most displeased. Straight away he called for forty barrels of wine to be consumed in a single draught.

Again the Fool was crestfallen. But the Thirsty Man cheered him up: 'I can drain them all in one go—and still have room for more.'

And so it was. The tsar was now growing desperate. He gave

orders for an iron bath-house to be heated until it was white hot; the Fool was to spend the night steaming himself in it—that would put paid to him, or so the tsar thought.

The Fool entered the bath-house, however, in the company of the Straw Man, who scattered his hay across the iron floor—to such effect that it became so cold that, barely had the Fool washed himself than the water turned to ice. When the tsar unlocked the bath-house next morning, out stepped the Fool, all washed and steamed, as fresh as a daisy.

That sent the tsar into a terrible rage; he locked himself in his royal chamber for several days before emerging with a new and cunning plan. The Fool was to assemble an entire regiment of soldiers by the morrow. Where would a simple peasant raise an army?

This is the end, thought the Fool. Turning to his companions, he thanked them for their help and was sorry their mission had been in vain.

'But you've forgotten me,' piped up the Brushwood Man. 'I can raise a mighty host in the twinkle of an eye. And if the tsar refuses to give up his daughter after that, our army will conquer his tsardom and take her by force!'

That night, the Fool's shipmate went into the royal meadow close by the palace, spread his brushwood over the grass and up sprang a vast army of cavalry, infantry, and artillery. When the tsar awoke next morning to behold this mighty force before his palace, he took fright and surrendered straight away.

At once he sent servants to the Fool, bearing furs and honey and precious gems. And he begged him to take the princess as his bride.

The Fool was clothed in rich velvet robes and became as handsome as the sky at dawn, the fairest man that ever was born. No one ever called him a fool after that; he grew wise and learned, much loved by all who met him—most of all by the fair princess.

Bella and the Bear

An old man and woman had a granddaughter whose name was Bella. And each summer she would stay with them in their tidy cottage beside a dark, dense forest. One summer's day the little girl's friends called on her to go mushrooming with them in the meadow.

'Granny, Grandad,' cried Bella. 'May I go out to play? I'll bring you lots of mushrooms, I promise.'

'Run along then,' the old pair said. 'But mind you don't go near the forest or the wolves or bears will get you.'

Off skipped the girls towards the meadow at the forest edge. Bella knew that the best and biggest mushrooms grew beneath the trees and bushes in the forest. Almost without noticing, she wandered out of sight of her friends. She moved from tree to tree, from bush to bush, filling her basket with mushrooms—browns and whites, reds and yellows.

All the while she was going deeper and deeper into the forest. Suddenly, she looked up and realized she was lost.

'Hell-ooooo! Hell-ooooo!' she called.

There was no reply.

But somebody did hear her!

From the trees came a rustling and a cracking, and out stepped a big brown bear. When he set eyes on the little girl, he threw up his arms in joy.

'Aha!' he cried. 'You'll make a fine servant for me, my pretty one.'

Taking the girl roughly by the arm, he dragged her to his cottage in the depths of the dark wood. Once inside, he growled at her, 'Now stoke the fire, cook some porridge, and make my home clean and tidy.'

There now began a miserable life in the bear's cottage for poor Bella. Day after day she toiled from dawn to dusk, afraid the bear would eat her. All the while she thought of how she could escape.

Finally, an idea came to her.

'Mister Bear,' she said politely, 'may I go home for a day to show my grandparents I'm alive and well?'

'Certainly not,' growled the bear. 'You'll never leave here. If you have a message for them, I'll take it myself.'

That was just what Bella had planned. She baked some cherry pies, piled them high upon a dish and fetched a big basket. Then she called the bear.

'Mister Bear, I'll put the pies in this basket for you to carry home. Remember though, don't open the basket and don't touch the pies. I'll be keeping my eye on you from the cottage roof.'

'All right, my pretty one,' grumbled the bear. 'Just let me take a nap before I go.'

No sooner was the bear asleep than Bella quickly climbed on to the roof and made a lifelike figure out of a pole, her coat and headscarf. Then she scrambled down, squeezed into the basket and pulled the dish of cherry pies over her head. When the bear awoke and saw the basket ready, he hoisted it on to his broad back and set off for the village.

Through the trees he ambled with his load and soon felt tired and footsore. Stopping by a tree stump, he sank down to rest, thinking to eat a cherry pie. But just as he was about to open the basket, he heard Bella's voice.

'Don't sit there all day and don't you touch those pies.'

Glancing round he could just see her figure on his roof.

'My, my, that maid has sharp eyes,' he muttered to himself.

Up he got and continued on his way.

On and on he went, carrying the heavy load. Soon he came upon another tree stump.

I'll just take a little rest and eat a cherry pie, he thought, puffing and panting with the weight.

Yet once again Bella's muffled voice was heard.

'Don't sit down and don't you touch those pies. Go straight to the village as I told you.'

He looked back, but could no longer see his house.

'Well, I'm blowed,' he exclaimed. 'She's got eyes like a hawk, that girl.'

So on he went.

Through the trees he shuffled, down into the valley, on through groves of ash, up grassy knolls until, finally, he emerged into a meadow.

'I must rest my poor feet,' he sighed. 'And I'll just have one small pie to refresh me. She surely cannot see me now.'

But from out of nowhere came a distant voice.

'I can see you. I can see you! Don't you touch those cherry pies. Go on, go on, go on.'

The bear was puzzled, even scared.

'What big eyes she has,' he growled, hurrying across the field.

At last he arrived at the village, stopped at Bella's door, and knocked loudly.

'Open up, open up!' he cried gruffly. 'I've brought a gift from your granddaughter.'

The moment they heard his voice, however, all the dogs of the village came running from their yards. Their barking startled him so much, he left the basket at the door and made off for the forest without a backward glance.

How surprised Bella's grandparents were when they opened the door to find the basket and no one in sight.

Grandad lifted up the lid, stared hard and could scarcely believe his eyes. For there beneath the cherry pies sat the little girl, alive and well.

Granny and Grandad both danced with joy, hugged Bella and said what a clever girl she was to trick the bear. Soon all her friends heard the news and came running to hug and kiss her too. Bella was so happy.

In the meantime, deep in the forest the old bear reached home and shouted to the figure on the roof to make his tea. Of course, it did not take him long to learn that the wise young girl had tricked him and got away.

The Frog Princess

Long ago, there lived a king and queen with their three sons. When the princes were grown to manhood, the king called them to him, saying, 'My dear sons, it is time for you to wed; let each take a bow and shoot an arrow. The maiden who returns your arrow shall be your bride.'

The three princes bowed low before the king and, each taking a single shaft, drew back the bowstring to loose an arrow.

The first son's arrow landed in a nobleman's garden and was returned by his daughter.

The second son's arrow landed in a merchant's garden and was returned by his daughter.

As for the third son, Prince Ivan, he shot his arrow so high and

wide that he quite lost sight of it. After searching half the day he finally found the arrow in a woodland pond; and sitting on a water lily holding the arrow in her mouth was a slimy frog. When Prince Ivan asked for it back, the frog replied, 'I shall return your arrow when you make me your bride.'

'But how can a prince marry a frog!' said Ivan in disgust.

The prince was angry, yet he could not disobey his father; so he picked up the frog and took her to the palace.

When he recounted the story to the king and showed him the frog, the monarch declared, 'My son, if the fates would have you wed a frog, so be it.'

Thus it was that three weddings were celebrated that Sunday: the first son married the nobleman's daughter, the second the merchant's daughter, and poor Ivan the frog.

Some time passed, and the king summoned his sons again and said, 'My dear sons, I wish to see which wife can make me the finest shirt; let each sew me a shirt by morning.'

The princes bowed low and went their separate ways. The two

eldest were not in the least dismayed, for they knew their wives could sew, but the youngest came home sad and sorrowful.

'Why do you hang your noble head, Prince Ivan?' croaked the frog-wife, hopping up to him.

'Well I might be downcast,' he replied. 'The king would have you sew him a shirt by morning.'

'Oh, is that all!' croaked the frog-wife. 'Eat your supper and go to bed. Morning is wiser than evening.'

As soon as Prince Ivan was asleep, the frog-wife hopped through the door and on to the porch, cast off her frog skin and turned into a princess fair beyond compare. Clapping her hands, she cried:

'Maids and nannies, heed my call,
Sew me a shirt like my father wore.'

At dawn, when Prince Ivan awoke, the frog was sitting upon the table beside a shirt all wrapped in an embroidered cloth. Overjoyed, he took the shirt to his father who was busy receiving the elder sons' gifts. The first son laid out his shirt before the king, who took it up and gruffly said, 'This shirt isn't fit for a peasant.'

The second son laid out his shirt before the king, and the monarch grumbled, 'This shirt isn't fit for a tinker.'

Then Prince Ivan laid out his shirt, so handsomely embroidered in silver and gold that the king's eyes sparkled with delight.

'Now here's a shirt fit for a king,' he exclaimed.

The three princes went their separate ways, with the two eldest muttering to each other, 'We were wrong to mock Prince Ivan's wife; she must be a wily witch for sure.'

By and by, the king summoned his sons again.

'My dear sons,' he said, 'your wives are to bake me a loaf of bread by morning; we'll see who is the finest cook.'

Again Prince Ivan left the palace sad and sorrowful, and his frog-wife asked him, 'Why do you hang your noble head, Prince Ivan?'

And he told her of the king's command.

'Oh, is that all?' she croaked. 'Eat your supper and go to bed. Morning is wiser than evening.'

Meanwhile the two eldest brothers sent an old woman from the palace kitchens to see how the frog baked her bread. But the frog-wife guessed what they were up to; she kneaded some dough, rolled it out, and tossed it straight into the oven fire.

Straightaway the old woman hurried back to the brothers to tell the news. And their wives proceeded to do as the frog had done.

No sooner had the woman gone, however, than the frog-wife hopped out of the door and on to the porch, cast off her frog skin and turned into a princess fair beyond compare. Clapping her hands, she called:

> 'Maids and nannies, bake bread so sweet,
> Just like my father used to eat.'

Next morning, when Prince Ivan awoke, he was overjoyed to find the crisp loaf of bread wrapped up in a fresh white cloth. Taking it to his father he watched as the king inspected his brothers' loaves.

First the king took the eldest son's loaf, which was all black and lumpy from the oven fire.

The king sent it crossly to the kitchens.

Then he inspected the second son's loaf, which was also charred and knobbly from the oven fire. And it too was despatched to the kitchens.

But when Prince Ivan handed him his loaf of bread, all crisp and brown, the king was so delighted he exclaimed, 'Now here's a loaf to grace the royal table.'

At once the king invited his three sons to bring their wives to a banquet that very evening. He wished to judge which wife could dance the best.

Once more Prince Ivan returned to his frog-wife with head bent low.

'Why do you hang your noble head, Prince Ivan?' croaked the frog.

He told her of the king's command.

'Do not grieve, Prince Ivan,' she said. 'This is what you must do: go to the banquet alone, I'll follow later. When you hear thunder, tell the guests it is your frog-wife arriving in her coach.'

So Prince Ivan went to the banquet by himself, while his elder brothers arrived with their wives dressed in all their finery.

The king and queen, their sons and wives and all the noble guests were just sitting down to dine when all of a sudden thunder boomed and the whole palace shook. But Prince Ivan calmed the guests, 'Fear not, good people, it is my wife arriving in her coach.'

At that moment, his wife entered: a beautiful princess dressed in a blue silk gown that glittered with silver stars; she wore the bright crescent moon in her golden hair. Her beauty was greater than tales can tell or words can relate. Prince Ivan was overjoyed, and the guests stared in awe at such finery.

As the meal proceeded the eldest brothers' wives noticed the frog princess slipping the roast swan bones into her right sleeve, and the last dregs of wine from her goblet into the left sleeve.

They followed suit: bones in one sleeve, drops of wine in the other.

When dinner was over, the king commanded the ball to commence. And the frog princess began to dance. She whirled round and round as the guests stood back and marvelled: when she shook her left sleeve a shimmering lake appeared; and when she shook her right sleeve a flight of white swans swam upon the lake.

The noble guests were filled with wonder.

Then the wives of the two elder sons began to dance. When they waved their arms, their wet sleeves flapped against the king's red face and bones flew out, hitting him in the eye. The king was most displeased and left the ball in a rage.

Prince Ivan, meanwhile, was overjoyed to find that his wife was a wise and lovely princess. But, fearing she would turn back into a frog, he slipped out of the palace and hurried home; taking up the frog-skin, he threw it into the oven fire.

When his wife returned and found her frog-skin gone, she burst into tears.

'Oh, Prince Ivan, what have you done!' she cried. 'Had you waited just three days more, we could have been happy forever. Now we have to part. If you wish to find me, you must journey beyond the Land of One Score and Nine to the realm of Old Bones the Dread.'

So saying, she turned into a grey cuckoo and flew out of the window.

A year went by, and Prince Ivan still pined for his wife. As a second year began, he took his father's blessing and set out to seek his wife.

Whether he walked high or low I do not know, far or near I did not hear, long time or less I cannot guess, but his boots were soon worn, his caftan torn, and his face forlorn.

One day, when he had almost lost all hope, he wandered into a forest glade and there spied a wooden hut on hen's feet, turning round and round.

'Little hut, little hut,' he called, 'turn your back to the trees and your face to me, please.'

At once the hut stopped turning, and a door opened for him to enter. As he crossed the threshold he saw an old woman who asked whither he was bound.

'I am searching for my frog-princess, Granny,' he replied, telling her his story.

Baba Yagá shook her head and sighed, 'Oh, Prince Ivan, why did you burn the frog skin? Yelena the Wise, for that is your frog-wife, grew up cleverer than her father, a mighty king; this angered him so much that he turned her into a frog for three years on her fourteenth birthday.'

'Granny, I'll do anything to find her,' said the sad prince.

'Old Bones the Dread now has her in his power,' continued Baba Yagá, 'and it will not be easy to rescue her, since no one has been able to slay him. His death is at the end of a needle, the needle is in an egg, the egg is in a duck, the duck is in a hare, the hare is in a stone chest, and the chest is at the top of a tall oak tree that Old Bones guards like the apple of his eye.

'Now take this ball of thread,' the old witch said, 'and follow wherever it rolls.'

Thanking Baba Yagá for her help, Prince Ivan rolled the ball of thread before him and followed it into the forest. It rolled on and on, finally emerging into a clearing where the prince saw a big brown bear. He was about to loose an arrow at it when the bear hailed him in a human voice, 'Do not slay me, Prince Ivan, you may have need of me some day.'

The prince took pity on the bear and continued on his way. A little further on he spotted a white drake flying overhead. He was about to shoot it when it cried out in a human voice, 'Do not shoot me, Prince Ivan, you may have need of me some day.'

So the prince spared the drake and journeyed on. Presently, a cross-eyed hare dashed across the prince's path: the prince took aim quickly and was about to shoot when the hare spoke up in a human voice, 'Do not kill me, Prince Ivan, you may have need of me some day.'

So Prince Ivan spared the hare's life and followed the ball of thread until he came to a lake; and there he found a pike lying on the bank, gasping for air.

'Take pity on me, Prince Ivan,' gasped the fish. 'Throw me back into the lake, for one day you may need me.'

So Prince Ivan threw the pike into the water and walked on, following the ball of thread.

Late that evening he came to the oak tree, standing tall and strong, the stone chest in the topmost branches well out of reach.

How would he bring it down?

The prince was in despair when, suddenly, from out of nowhere, the big brown bear appeared; it went up to the tree, grasped the trunk in its sturdy arms and pulled it up by the roots. Down crashed the

chest on to the ground and split asunder, so loosing a hare which bounded away as fast as it could.

At that moment, a cross-eyed hare appeared and gave chase, catching the first and tearing it to pieces.

Out of the dead hare flew a duck that flapped up into the sky. In a trice the white drake was upon it and struck it so hard that it dropped an egg. Down fell the egg into a nearby lake.

At that, Prince Ivan wept in despair: how would he find the egg at the bottom of the lake?

Imagine his joy when the pike came swimming to the shore with the egg in its mouth. The prince cracked open the egg, took out the needle and began to bend it.

The more it bent, the more Old Bones the Dread writhed and twisted in his palace of black stone. And when Prince Ivan broke off the end of the needle, Old Bones fell down dead.

As the prince turned about, there was Yelena the Wise standing before him.

'Oh, Prince Ivan,' she sighed, 'how long you were in coming. I almost had to wed Old Bones the Dread who held me in his power.'

Reunited at last, the prince and princess returned to Rus and lived there long and happily.

The Rosy Apple
and the Golden Bowl

*There once lived an old man and woman with
their three daughters. The two eldest girls were vain
and cruel, but the third, Tania, was quiet and
modest in all she did.*

The eldest girls were also lazy and stupid, sitting at home all day,
while Tania busied herself in the house and garden from dawn to
dusk.

One day, the old man made ready to take hay to market,
promising to bring back presents for each of his daughters.

'Buy me a length of silk, father,' said the first girl.

'Buy me a length of red velvet,' said the second.

Tania said nothing.

The old man asked again.

'Come now, what shall I fetch you, my child?'

'Bring me a rosy apple and a golden bowl,' she said at last.

At that her sisters laughed so hard they nearly split their sides.

'How silly you are,' they cried. 'Why, we have a whole orchard of apples, you can pick as many as you please. As for a bowl, what do you want that for? To feed the ducks from?'

'No, dear sisters. I shall roll the apple in the bowl and say some magic words. An old beggar-woman once told me them for giving her a cake.'

Her sisters laughed even louder, and their father reproached them:

'Now, now, that's enough. I'll bring presents for all of you.'

The old man sold his hay and purchased all three gifts.

The two eldest sisters were delighted with their presents and at once set to making new dresses, all the while poking fun at their sister.

'Sit there and roll your apple, stupid!' they called.

Tania sat quietly in a corner, rolling her rosy apple in the golden bowl, singing softly to herself:

'Rosy apple, roll, roll
Round my little golden bowl.
Show me meadows and seas
And forests and leas,
And mountains so high
They reach to the sky.'

Suddenly, bells began to ring and light flooded the whole cottage. Round and round the golden bowl rolled the rosy apple and there appeared in the bowl, as clear as day, downs and dales, soldiers in fields with swords and shields, grassy leas and ships on seas, and mountains so high they reached to the sky.

The two eldest sisters could hardly believe their eyes. Their only thought was to take the apple and bowl from their sister.

Tania, however, would not exchange her present, she never let the apple and bowl out of her sight, and would play with them every evening.

One day, tired of waiting, the two wicked sisters decided to lure her into the forest.

'Come, sweet sister,' they said. 'Let us go and pick some berries and flowers in the woods.'

But there were no berries or flowers anywhere to be seen. So Tania took out her golden bowl and rolled the rosy apple in it as she sang softly:

> 'Rosy apple, roll, roll
> Round the little golden bowl.
> Show me strawberry red and cornflower blue,
> Poppies and daisies and violets too.'

At once bells began to peal and there appeared strawberry red and cornflower blue, poppies and daisies and violets too.

As Tania's two cruel sisters watched, a wicked gleam came into their eyes. While their sister sat quietly on a log, staring down at her golden bowl, they killed her with a knife and buried her body beneath a silver birch tree. Then they took the rosy apple and golden bowl for themselves.

It was evening by the time they reached home, bringing baskets piled high with berries and flowers. They told their parents, 'Tania ran away from us and was lost. We searched everywhere for her, but could not find her. Wolves or bears must have eaten her.'

On hearing that, the mother burst into tears, and the father said grimly, 'Roll the apple round the bowl, perhaps it will show us where Tania is.'

The sisters turned cold with fear, but they had to do as their father said. Yet when they tried to roll the apple in the bowl, it would not roll, and the bowl would not spin. The wicked sisters breathed a sigh of relief.

Not long after, a young shepherd was wandering through the woods, looking for a stray sheep; and he came upon a silver birch with a fresh green mound beneath it and blue cornflowers glowing all around. Long, slender reeds were shooting up amidst the flowers and from one of these he cut himself a pipe to play.

No sooner had he put the pipe to his lips than it started to play by itself. And these were the words it sang:

'Play, pipe, play, for my father to hear,
Play, pipe, play for my father to cheer.
By my sisters I did die,
Beneath the silver birch I lie.'

When the news reached Tania's father he asked the shepherd to take him to where he cut his pipe. So the shepherd led him to the fresh green mound in the forest where blue cornflowers were growing beneath the silver birch tree. Together they dug a hole and found Tania in her shallow grave, quite cold and dead; she looked more lovely than ever, as if she were in peaceful sleep.

Suddenly, the pipe began to play again.

'Play, pipe, play, songs sad and gay,
Listen, father, to what I say:
Everything to you I'll tell
If you fetch water from the royal well.'

At these words, the two wicked sisters trembled and paled, fell to their knees and confessed their crime. Without more ado the old man set out for the royal palace to fetch the water.

When he finally reached the palace, he told the king his story and soon gained the king's assent to take water from his well. On returning to his daughter with a flask of water, he sprinkled her fair brow with it. At once Tania stirred, opened her eyes and hugged her mother and father.

She was as lovely as the flowers in spring, her eyes were as radiant as the rays of the sun, her face was as fair as the sky at dawn, and the tears rolling down her cheeks were like the purest pearls.

As for the wicked sisters, they were summoned to the king and he would have had them put to death for their evil crime. But at Tania's pleading, he had them banished to a bleak island at the other end of the land.

Tania, meanwhile, married the handsome shepherd who had first found her grave beneath the silver birch tree. And from then on the forest was known as Holy Wood.

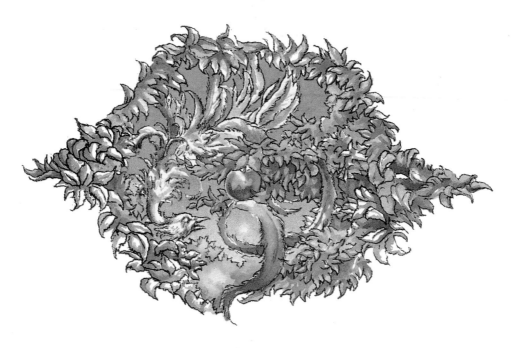

The Firebird

Across the misty mountains, over deep rolling seas,
there lived a king who had an orchard that was the
apple of his eye. For in the orchard grew a
golden apple tree.

But a thief came and stole some apples in the night.

The king was most upset. He set his stable lad to stand guard all night.

Half the night passed and then, all of a sudden, it grew as light as day. The lad, Ivan, looked up and there, in the apple tree, he saw a firebird, biting and bolting as bold as brass.

Quickly climbing up the tree, he grabbed the firebird's tail. But it tore free and flew away, leaving a feather in Ivan's hand. Next morning, he showed the king his prize. The feather lit up the room in a fiery glow!

'Ivan,' the monarch said, 'you must fetch the firebird and catch the thief.'

Ivan bowed low, prepared some bread and cheese and beer, then set off he knew not where.

He was wandering through a forest when a big grey wolf suddenly appeared.

'Sit upon my back,' the grey wolf said, 'and I'll help you find the thief.'

Ivan did as he was told and they sped off as swiftly as the wind. Fields swept by in the wink of an eye, lakes skimmed past very fast and, in a trice, they came to a sunlit glade upon a hill.

'Now heed what I say,' said the wolf. 'Mix your beer with bread and cheese and scatter it on the ground. Then hide behind a tree.'

Ivan did as he was told; then he and the wolf hid behind the trees. By and by, in the gathering gloom the glade gleamed and glowed in a blaze of light.

The firebirds were coming!

Like trailing stars, they swooped upon the beer-soaked bread; and in no time at all they were reeling about in rickety rings. From behind a tree, Ivan stood and stared. The firebirds were four times bigger than the cocks at home, and their tails blazed brighter than a thousand fires.

Creeping up behind them, he swiftly seized a firebird by the tail, thrust it in a sack and leapt upon the grey wolf's back. And off they swept like the wind.

At last they reached the king; Ivan set down his sack upon the floor and untied the neck. A flood of light lit up the room, and the king shut tight his eyes in fear.

'Oh dear, oh dear, we're all on fire!' he wailed. 'Call out the fire brigade.'

'This is no fire, sire,' laughed Ivan. 'I've brought the firebird.'

'Oh, my darling boy,' the king declared, peering through his thumbs. 'So it is, so it is! A thousand thanks.'

But the king was not entirely content. Perhaps Ivan could do him another turn?

Now, the king was fond of fairy tales and had heard of a princess, Yelena the Fair, who lived beyond the seas.

'Fetch her here,' said the king. 'I'll make her my wife.'

With bowed head, Ivan returned to the grey wolf, reporting the king's command.

'Come, climb on my back,' the grey wolf said.

And off raced the wolf with Ivan clinging to its neck. Whether they were long on their way I cannot say; but by and by they came to a fairy-tale castle beyond the seas.

'Leave this to me,' said the wolf.

While Ivan waited beside an oak, the wolf sprang over the castle wall and, in no time at all, was back with Yelena the Fair across his back.

'Now mount up behind the fair princess,' said the wolf, 'and hang on tight.'

It was not long before they were back in the old king's realm. But before they could deliver the stolen bride, Ivan said with tears in his eyes, 'Oh, big grey wolf, I have fallen in love with Yelena the Fair, and she with me. What are we to do?'

'Leave it to me,' the wolf replied. 'I'll turn myself into the living likeness of the fair princess; then you take me to the king.'

Turning head over heels and back to front, the wolf changed himself into the very likeness of Yelena the Fair. At once, Ivan led the wolf-princess to the aged king.

The king was overjoyed. He summoned his nobles to celebrate the crowning of his new queen. But just as he went to kiss the bride— Oh dear me!—his lips met the muzzle of the big grey wolf!

The shock was too severe. The old king died upon the spot.

As the wolf ran off, Yelena the Fair herself appeared, leading Ivan by the hand.

'As I am now your queen,' she said, addressing the gathered guests, 'I'm making Ivan the king.'

So Ivan married Yelena the Fair; and together they ruled in peace and cheer for many a long and happy year.

As for the firebird—can you guess? They set it free to fly away; but never again did it nibble at apples or bread and cheese.

About these stories

During my five years in Russia, I would seek out storytellers in their cosy wooden shacks and we would swap yarns, riddles, tongue-twisters, and songs ('Old Macdonald Had a Farm' was my stock-in-trade!) over a steaming bowl of soup. Sometimes near Moscow, sometimes in the Ural Mountains, sometimes in Yakutia in far-off Siberia—for Russia is the largest land in the world.

What a wonderful setting for a fairy tale. In the midst of the dense forest, with trees crackling from the frost, to the accompaniment of wolves howling, beside a blazing fire, an entire village would listen to the storyteller . . . and believe every word.

It was a reminder of an age before television, newspapers, and schools, when stories bound the people together and brought hope of a better life. Picture the scene as you read these stories.

In a dungeon deep a princess pines
A big grey wolf his captive minds;
There, Baba Yagá in her mortar looms
Sweeping her traces away with her brooms;
There, Old Bones the Ogre hoards his gold,
There's Russian blood, there's Rus so old.

James Riordan
1999

Notes on the stories

Vasilissa the Wise and Baba Yagá

The witch (Baba Yagá) here symbolizes the dark cloud that wants to destroy the sunlight (Vasilissa). The sun, however, manages to free itself from the power of the storm and other dark clouds (the stepmother and her daughters).

Ivan the Fool and the Magic Pike

The youngest son was originally the heir in Russia, a position which he gradually lost with changing social conditions. So he is often regarded as an heir deprived of his rights and therefore someone to sympathize with. In the Russian village generally, there was also a toleration, even veneration, of the simple-minded as saintly people.

The Animals' Revenge

The hero of many Russian animal tales is the crafty, resourceful fox, variously known as the beautiful vixen, the gossip, godmother, little sister, mother-confessor, a deceiving midwife. Unlike most Western tales (Reynard the Fox or Brer Fox), the Russian fox is female—an indication of the proximity of Russian tales to the Matriarchal Age.

Snowmaiden

This story is a Russian mythological representation of the changing seasons. It is one of the oldest of all folk-tales, featuring pagan characters like Yarilo the Sun God. In Russian custom to this day, Grandfather Frost (*Ded Moroz*) is Father Christmas, while Snowmaiden (*Snegurochka*) is his handmaiden who distributes the presents.

Fenist the Falcon

In Russian mythology, when Fenist (a corruption of 'Phoenix') is awoken by a maiden's kiss, it is really Nature being awoken by spring, the earth being kissed by the sun. In contrast to Western tales, here the prince is awoken by a woman.

The Flying Ship

This is another example of the Fool, the youngest son, the idle daydreamer, who makes his fortune with the aid of helpful companions. He also turns out to be wise and loved by all, including the fair princess.

Bella and the Bear

Here again it is an enterprising young girl who gets the better of a (male) animal. In most Russian animal tales, the bear, Misha, is the twig-crusher, the old grey peasant, clumsy and slow-witted, but also sometimes kind-hearted.

The Frog Princess

Once more we have an example of the differences in the treatment of women as folk-tale characters. In the West European story, the frog is a prince; here it is a princess.

The Rosy Apple and the Golden Bowl
This story brings us to another element of
Russian primitive belief: that the soul or
heart dwelt outside the body in some special
place. Here a tree is tenanted by the soul of
the dead girl. This superstition led to certain
trees being regarded as sacred.

The Firebird

There are many versions of tales featuring
the mythical firebird—on whom the
composer Igor Stravinsky based his ballet
of the same name.

Sources

Unless otherwise indicated, all stories are taken from Afanasiev, *Narodnye russkie skazki A.N. Afanasieva v tryokh tomakh*, (Moscow, 1957).
'Vasilissa the Wise', vol. 1, no. 104, pp. 159–66.
'Ivan the Fool', vol. 1, nos. 165–8, pp. 401–15.
'The Animals' Revenge', vol. 1, nos. 1–7, pp. 3–15, and nos. 40–3, pp. 59–64.
'Snowmaiden', Alexei Tolstoy, vol. 5, pp. 331–40.
'Fenist the Falcon', *Skazki A.N. Korolkovoi*, (Voronezh, 1941).
'The Flying Ship', vol. 1, no. 144, pp. 315–19.
'Bella and the Bear', K.D. Ushinsky, *Rodnoye slovo*, vol. 6, pp. 152–5.
'The Frog Princess', vol. 2, no. 267, pp. 311–19.
'The Rosy Apple and the Golden Bowl', A.N. Nechayev, *Russkie skazki*, (Moscow, 1970), pp. 50–5.
'The Firebird', vol. 1, nos. 168–70, pp. 415–31.